W9-BXU-788

This book belongs to:

_____

_____

_____

First published by Walker Books Ltd.,
87 Vauxhall Walk, London SE11 5HJ

First U.S. edition 2012

Library of Congress Cataloging-in-Publication Data is available.
Library of Congress Catalog Card Number pending
ISBN 978-0-7636-5883-0

12 13 14 15 16 17 CCP 10 9 8 7 6 5 4 3 2 1

Printed in Shenzhen, Guangdong, China

This book was typeset in Lucy Cousins.
The illustrations were done in gouache.

Candlewick Press
99 Dover Street
Somerville, Massachusetts 02144

visit us at www.candlewick.com

Maisy Goes on a Sleepover

Lucy Cousins

CANDLEWICK PRESS

One day at the playground, Tallulah gave Maisy a card. It was an invitation to a sleepover.

Maisy had never been on a sleepover before. She was excited to go on her first one!

At home, Maisy started packing. What would she need? Pajamas, toothbrush, a sleeping bag, clean clothes for the morning. Panda would come, too, of course!

Then Maisy and Panda
went to Tallulah's house.

"Welcome to my sleepover,"
Tallulah said. "Come inside!"

"Meet my new friend, Ella,"
Tallulah said. "She is sleeping
over, too." Ella had been on a
sleepover before.

Maisy felt a little shy but she and
Panda liked Ella very much.
They couldn't wait to
play together.

Then Tallulah
put on some music,

and Ella did a dance,

Maisy felt a little shy but she and
Panda liked Ella very much.
They couldn't wait to
play together.

Then Tallulah
put on some music,

and Ella did a dance,

which made
everyone laugh.

They all tried it.
They called it
Ella's **Twist**
and **Spin**.

Next it was time for Tallulah's special sleepover supper.

There were sandwiches and fruit, with cupcakes and ice cream for dessert. Ooh! It was delicious!

Afterward, they played games:
jump rope, tag,

and hide-and-seek.

Next they laid out their sleeping bags. It was strange getting ready for bed at Tallulah's house.

Then Ella bounced on the bed and everyone laughed again.

They put
on their
pajamas,

then went to
the bathroom
and brushed
their teeth.

Everyone got into bed.
Maisy read a bedtime
story, but no one felt
like sleeping yet. They
laughed and talked
for a long time.

Maisy told Panda that she thought sleepovers were lots of fun and that maybe next time she would invite everyone to her house.

At last, everyone
fell asleep. Good night,
Maisy. Good night, Panda.
Good night, everyone!
Sweet dreams...

See you in the morning!